For Jim,
May the poetry
never end . . .
—JBG

For
aspiring poets
everywhere
—K.B.

Amazon Publishing
Attn: Amazon Children's Publishing
P.O. Box 400818, Las Vegas, NV 89140
www.amazon.com/amazonchildrenspublishing

Library of Congress Cataloging-in-Publication Data is available upon request.

ISBN-13: 9781477847152 (hardcover)
ISBN-10: 1477847154 (hardcover)
ISBN-13: 9781477897157 (eBook)
ISBN-10: 1477897151 (eBook)

Editor: Melanie Kroupa
Design by Ryan Michaels
Printed in Mexico (R)

FIRST EDITION
10 9 8 7 6 5 4 3 2 1

THE POEM THAT WILL NOT END

It started with a rhythm,
a rhythm and a rhyme.
It wouldn't let me stop,
it ate up all my time.

Beat
Feet meet
Repeat
~~Repeat~~

rhyme
time
~~time~~
~~time~~

feet
beat
repeat
sweet

Rhythm

I was seized by a rhythmical beat,
It was something I could not delete.
I went crazy with rhyme.
It just gobbled my time.
Had me clapping and tapping my feet.

I tried to eat my breakfast
but didn't hesitate
to scribble on the napkins
and doodle cross my plate.

GOING BANANAS

Baby brother loves to smear
banana every place,
then squeeze it through his fingers
and wipe it on his face.
He blows banana bubbles
and makes banana goo—
oh yuck, ugh, ew, what a mess!
I'd like to do that, too.

And, when we hit the playground,
I scratched words in the dirt.

THE BASEBALL GAME

The kids creamed the teachers,
    listen to the score:
The third graders beat them—
    twenty-five to four!

We got them out at second,
    we caught their pop flies.
We got them out at home plate,
    much to their surprise.

When we scored all the home runs,
    we screamed and made a fuss.
We may get Ds in English,
    but in baseball we're A+!

Then in the cafeteria—
with just two tasty tries—
between my lunch and Aimee's,
I wrote two lines with fries.

COUPLET FOR FRENCH FRIES
Two lines are not enough to express
How much I adore your potato-ness

I ran outside at recess,
pulled out a piece of chalk,
didn't waste a minute—
dashed poems on the walk.

CAPTURED

I'm captured, won't you help me find a way,
to free me from this urgent need to write?
It follows me and hounds me night and day.
I'm captured, won't you help me find a way,
to toss aside this curse—I want to play!
You must admit . . . this is a scary sight.
I'm captured, won't you help me find a way,
to free me from this urgent need to write?

I beg you, won't you help me?
Please help me, be a friend.
Rescue me, I'm captured—
this poem will not end!

The bell rang and I bolted,
wasn't running out of steam.
I wrote with mud out in the yard—
chased by the soccer team.

SOCCER BALL

Soccer ball,
you are the center,
sun of our universe.
We are planets orbiting
your supreme presence,
hoping to rocket you,
like a blazing comet,
into the galaxy of
our goal.

I ran right home and grabbed my bike.
Can I escape this curse?
My wheels were doing curlicues
and writing lines of verse.

BIKE

step on—
I am wheels
and gears,
I am speed.
I will heed
your slightest
command.

I will take you
anywhere.
I am wind
in your hair,
I am things
unsaid,
I'm the road
ahead . . . .

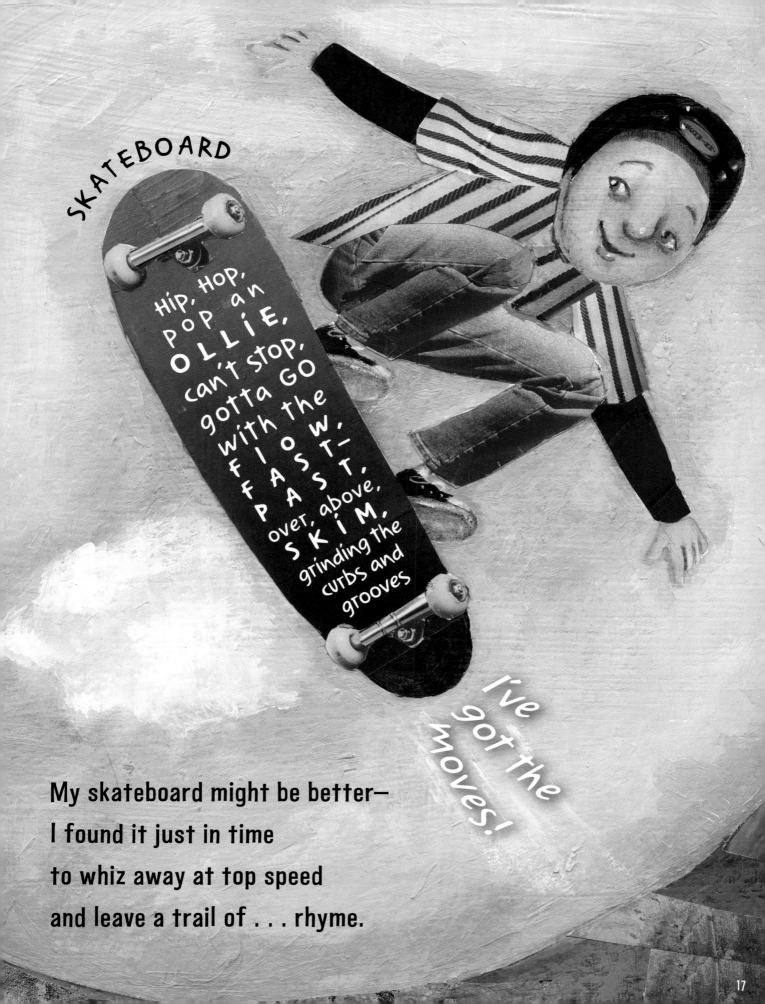

SKATEBOARD

Hip, Hop, pop an OLLiE, can't stop, gotta GO with the flow. FAST-FAST, over, above, SKIM, grinding the curbs and grooves

I've got the moves!

My skateboard might be better—
I found it just in time
to whiz away at top speed
and leave a trail of . . . rhyme.

PEAS

My mouth is filled with peas,
No matter how I wheeze,
I can't hold back this S·N·E·E·Z·E!

Dinner was no different,
I had . . . I had to S-N-E-E-Z-E.
I looked up at the kitchen wall
and saw three lines in . . . peas.

The ditty that I wrote that night
was delectable and meaty.
I inked with marker on my toes,
a new kind of gra-FEET-i.

FEET

My feet—
they can't stay still.
They are always moving
to some cool rhythm I hear in
my head.

Used pick-up-sticks for limericks,
wrote cinquain in the rain,
stacked sonnets up the staircase—
good grief, this is insane.

CONDUCTOR

In storms I can conduct a symphony:
I stand in front of all those instruments,
And, wow, I feel excited—what suspense—
As all those sounds become a part of me.

I play the wind, the thunder, and the sea!
I am in charge, this power is intense—
A world of rhythm that is huge, immense,
It swirls about me wild and mightily!

I get to choose the singer and the song.
With my baton I tell them when to start.
We work together great and I belong;
It's fun to be the leader, be a part
Of all those sounds that sweep about so strong—
that echo in the drumming of my heart.

FEVER

I cannot stop this fever in my brain,
I feel compelled to write, and write, and write.
Day in, day out, the words just fall like rain.

Is there some way that I can plug the drain—
To rescue me, to save me from this plight?
I cannot stop this fever in my brain.

I've stepped on board a rhythm kind of train,
That's traveling, zooming at the speed of light
Day in, day out, the words just fall like rain.

What made this happen no one can explain,
I toss and turn and twist each sleepless night.
I cannot stop this fever in my brain.

What's that? You say that I should not complain?
I'm tired and hungry, but you might be right.
Day in, day out, the words just fall like rain.

Now, I just wrote this villanelle refrain.
Hey . . . maybe I should NOT put up a fight.
I cannot stop this fever in my brain.
Day in, day out, the words just fall like rain.

My brain went into overdrive,
I started writing faster,
careening wild at breakneck speed—
a poetry disaster.

My mom called up, "Are you in bed?"

but I could hardly hear her.

I'd found a tube of toothpaste

and was writing on the mirror.

HANDSOME

"You're handsome, smart, and wonderful;
you're special—like no other . . . ."

"Aw, you're just saying that . . .
you have to-you're my mother!"

I spent a restless night and thought,
Whatever can I do?

SLEEP

Why is it I can never remember the last moment before sleep?

GOOSE DOWN PILLOW

My head sinks into the feathered pillow; I think I hear geese whisper.

FISHING

There are poems that swim in my head,
They take form as I lie in my bed.
With my pen for a hook,
I might quick have a look,
And then catch them on paper instead.

When I woke up, I found my pillows covered with . . . haiku!

TIRED

I am so tired
I'm part
of the bed—
a cover pressed
against the sheets,
dangling limply
down the sides.

I dragged into the classroom
as the bell began to ring.

My teacher's next assignment!

Write a poem about "spring".

My spring was sprung with this assault—
my brain came grinding to a halt.
My mind became a total blank,

SPEECHLESS

Sometimes when I am
asked to speak, my tongue shrivels,
dries, and disappears,
and then my mouth becomes a
hollow bell with no ringer.

BLANK VERSE

I'm running out of steam—I've got to halt.
This inspiration spree has reached its end.
My fevered Brain Train screeches, brakes, and STOPS.
It pulls in, finds a track, where it can rest.

and I have dear Ms. Frost to thank!

P.S. I asked Ms. Frost, "Instead of the poem about 'Spring,'
can I turn in some of my 'recent work' if I write it on . . . paper?"
She said, "Yes." Ms. Frost is so-o cool! I even got an A+. Life is good.
To be more informed about poetic forms, I did some digging.

Here's what I discovered . . .

RYAN O'BRIAN'S GUIDE to POETIC FORMS

ACROSTIC: If you spell a word (It could be your name!) downward, you can use each of the letters as the beginning of a word or phrase. EXAMPLE: "RECESS," P. 12

BLANK VERSE: Blank verse is unrhymed iambic pentameter. To find out about that last part, keep reading. EXAMPLE: "BLANK VERSE," P. 27

CINQUAIN: Say SIN'-kane. The secret code for this poem is 2, 4, 6, 8, 2 (two syllables/beats on the first line, four beats on the next, then six beats, eight, and back to two beats in the last line). It's a building thought-wave that crashes and leaves some treasure. EXAMPLE: "FEET," P. 19

Wow

CONCRETE POEM: It's a picture poem that takes the shape of what it's about—word art, sculpting with words. Use simple shapes—make it easy to read.

Experiment on your computer. Try out different fonts to see which work best.

A major blast!

EXAMPLES: "SOCCER BALL," P. 15, "SKATEBOARD," P. 17

COUPLET: Two lines that usually rhyme. EXAMPLE: "COUPLET FOR FRENCH FRIES," P. 10

FOOT/FEET: Music has a beat, poetry has feet; each foot contains beats which are either stressed (ˊ) or unstressed (◡). Iambs (◡ˊ, "SUR-PRISE") and anapests (◡◡ˊ, "in my HEAD") have a rising rhythm; trochees (ˊ◡, "LIGHT-ning") and dactyls (ˊ◡◡, "RHYTH-mi-cal") have a falling rhythm. There are many other kinds of feet, but these are the most common.

FREE VERSE: A poem written without using a fixed, formal pattern of rhythm and rhyme.

EXAMPLES: "SOCCER BALL," P. 15, "TIRED," P. 25

HAIKU: A Japanese form which, in only 17 syllables (5-7-5), can create a feeling or paint a scene; usually it's about nature and is written now, in present tense; makes you say "Ah ha!" or "Oh, yeah!" EXAMPLES: "FOOTPRINTS," P. 8, "SLEEP," P. 24, AND "GOOSE DOWN PILLOW," P.24

LIMERICK: A funny five-line poem written in iambs and anapests; lines 1, 2, and 5 have three feet and rhyme, and lines 3 and 4 have two feet and rhyme. EXAMPLES: "RHYTHM," P. 5, "FISHING," P. 24, AND "ANONYMOUS," BACK COVER

PENTAMETER: Five feet to each line. EXAMPLES: "CAPTURED," P. 13, "CONDUCTOR," P. 20-21, "FEVER," P. 22, AND "BLANK VERSE," P. 27 ARE ALL WRITTEN IN IAMBIC PENTAMETER: "IN STORMS I CAN CONDUCT A SYMPHONY," ◡ˊ◡ˊ◡ˊ◡ˊ◡ˊ◡

QUATRAIN: A four-line stanza or poem that usually rhymes; code—abcb, abab, abba (The letters tell which lines rhyme with each other.). EXAMPLES: "GOING BANANAS," P. 7, AND "THE BASEBALL GAME," P. 9, BOTH HAVE abcb QUATRAINS.

RHYME: A repetition of sounds at the ends of words and usually at the end of a line: score/four, flies/surprise, fuss/A+ "The kids creamed the teachers,/ listen to the score:/ The third graders beat them—/ twenty-five to four!" No, a poem doesn't have to rhyme. Rhyme can boss you around—don't let it. And, please, **DO NOT** throw in any dumb word just to rhyme. EXAMPLES: "GOING BANANAS," P. 7, "THE BASEBALL GAME," P. 9, "PEAS," P. 18, AND "HANDSOME," P. 23, TO MENTION A FEW.

RHYTHM: Arrangement, flow, measured motion, regular beat of words, meter—learning to move to the groove.

SONNET: Was I channeling some 13th Century Italian poet? The code for this is abbaabba, cdecde, or cdcdcd. There is an octave (8 lines) and a sestet (6 lines). In the octave there are two envelope rhymes (that's the bb part) tucked into the middles. For a Shakespearean sonnet, the code is this: abab, cdcd, efef, gg. Both are 14 lines of iambic pentameter. EXAMPLE: "CONDUCTOR" IS AN ITALIAN SONNET—abbaabba cdcdcd, P. 20-21

STANZA: A pattern or grouping of lines in a poem—couplet (2 lines), tercet (3), quatrain (4), quintet (5), sestet (6), septet (7), octave (8).

TANKA: A Japanese form, which includes a haiku and adds two more seven-syllable lines to extend or change the meaning: 5-7-5-7-7 EXAMPLE: "SPEECHLESS," P. 27

TERCET: A three-line, usually rhyming, poem or stanza. EXAMPLE: "PEAS," P. 18

TRIOLET: This eight-line form has one line that repeats three times. Lines 1, 4, and 7 are the same; lines 2 and 8 also match. The first two lines become the last two lines. Got it? Code: abaaabab. EXAMPLE: "CAPTURED," P. 13

VILLANELLE: Written in iambic pentameter (◡′/◡′/◡′/◡′/◡′), a french form, usually five stanzas of three lines each with a final stanza of four lines. There are two strong repeating lines. To see the pattern of how this puzzle fits together look at "Fever." If you get two good repeating lines and two sets of words that have lots of rhymes, you can do this! EXAMPLE: "FEVER," P. 22

VOICES

You know how you can make your voice scary or funny?

Well, you can create different voices in poems, too.

NARRATIVE: A story-telling poem. EXAMPLES: "GOING BANANAS," P. 7, "THE BASEBALL GAME," P. 9

LYRICAL: Explore the music of words and individual feelings. In fact, the words to songs are called *lyrics*. *You* are an important part of this poem, and often pronouns such as *me, my,* and *I* are used. EXAMPLES: "CONDUCTOR," P. 20-21, "FEVER," P. 22

MASK: When you put on a mask, like at Halloween, and speak from the viewpoint of the object itself, you are using the mask or persona voice. EXAMPLE: "BIKE" (THE BIKE GETS TO TALK FOR ITSELF!), P. 16

APOSTROPHE (OR ADDRESS): This is a poem where you address or speak to something or someone who doesn't answer. EXAMPLE: "SOCCER BALL" (I LOVE TALKING *TO* THE SOCCER BALL!), P. 15

CONVERSATIONAL: In this voice at least two people or things are speaking with each other in a conversation. EXAMPLE: "HANDSOME," P. 23

Lots of great books can help you learn more about all the forms, voices, and choices you can try when you write your own poems. Check www.joangraham.com for a list.

Have FUN! Happy Reading! Happy Writing!

P.P.S. from Ryan: If you show your teacher

you wrote a VILLANELLE or a SONNET,

she is going to be so-o IMPRESSED.

She might even faint or give you extra

credit or both. You should definitely try it.